This Little Princess

story belongs to

. . . .

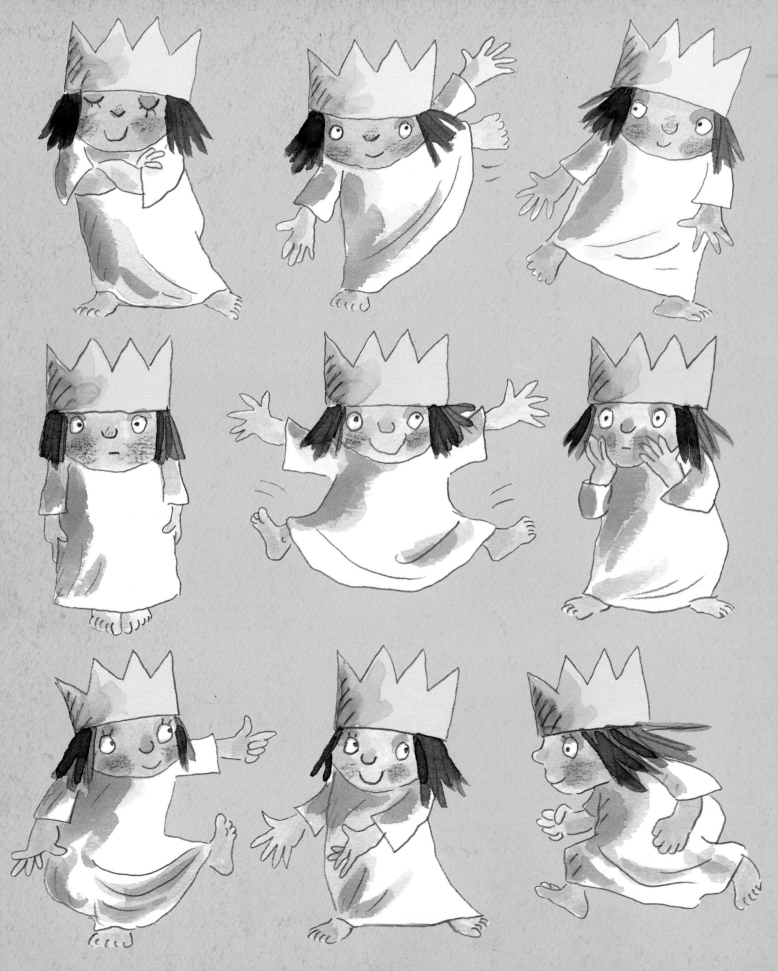

To Jackson

This paperback edition first published in 2014 by Andersen Press Ltd.,
20 Vauxhall Bridge Road, London SW1V 2SA.
Published in Australia by Random House Australia Pty.,
Level 3, 100 Pacific Highway, North Sydney, NSW 2060.
First published in Great Britain in 1987 by Andersen Press Ltd.
Copyright © Tony Ross, 2012
The rights of Tony Ross to be identified as the author and illustrator
of this work have been asserted by him in accordance with the
Copyright, Designs and Patents Act, 1988.
All rights reserved.
Colour separated in Switzerland by Photolitho AG, Zürich.
Printed and bound in Malaysia by Tien Wah Press.

10   9   8   7   6   5   4   3   2   1

British Library Cataloguing in Publication Data available.
ISBN 978 1 84939 764 3

A Little Princess Story

I Want a Boyfriend!

Tony Ross

Andersen Press

The Maid picked a flower and handed it to the General.

"Why did you do that?" said the Little Princess.
"Because he is my boyfriend," smiled the Maid.

"What's a boyfriend?" asked the Little Princess.
"He looks after me," said the Maid.

"I WANT A BOYFRIEND!" said the Little Princess.

"I am a PRINCESS and so I must be looked after."

"She wants a boyfriend!" cried the Maid.

"She wants a boyfriend!" said the General,
looking for one under a bush.

"She wants a BOYFRIEND!" said the Prime Minister
to the Teacher while looking in the waste paper basket.

"Donald will do," said the Teacher. "He is nice."

So Donald was made into the Royal Boyfriend,
and the Little Princess gave him a flower.

They gave each other flowers for two days.
"What else can we do?" asked Donald.

"Let's play house with Puss and Scruff," said the Little Princess.

"No, I don't like that!" said Donald.
"Let's go and jump over the stream."

"No, I don't like that!" said the Little Princess.
"Let's take Gilbert for a walk in the pram."

"No, I don't like that!" said Donald.
"Let's play football."

"No, I don't like football!" said the Little Princess.
"Let's pick some flowers."

"Oh NO!" said Donald. "Not flowers again.
Flowers are BORING!"

"So are you!" said the Little Princess.
"I don't like boys."

" . . . and I don't like GIRLS!" said Donald.

So Donald took his football and went home.

And the Little Princess went up to her bedroom
and pulled Gilbert out of the toy box.

"Will you be my boyfriend?" she smiled.

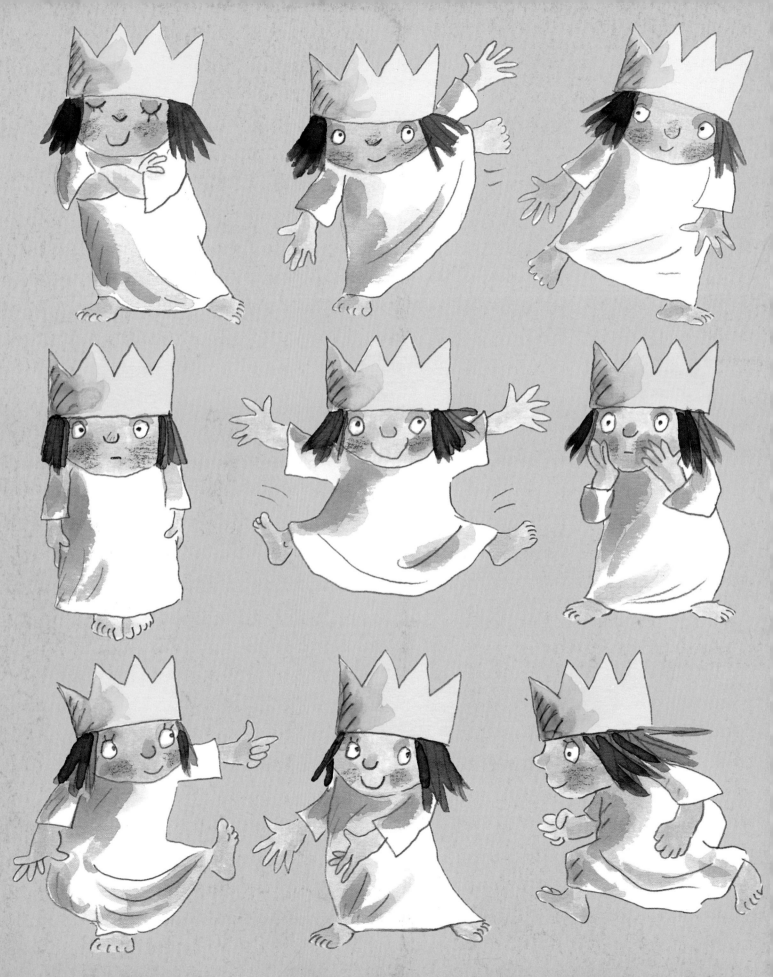

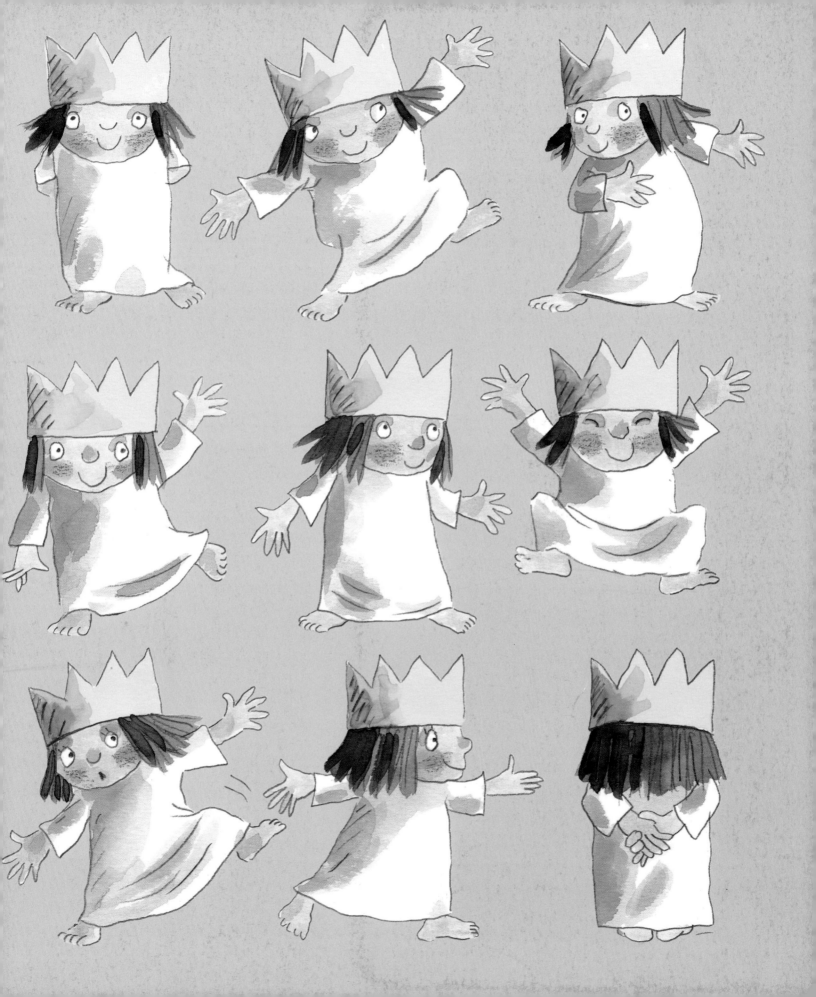

Other Little Princess Books

I Didn't Do it!

I Don't Want to Go to Hospital!

I Don't Want to Wash My Hands!

I Want a Boyfriend!

I Want a Party!

I Want a Sister!

I Want My Dummy!

I Want My Light On!

I Want My Potty!

I Want to Be!

I Want to Do it By Myself!

I Want to Go Home!

I Want to Win!

I Want Two Birthdays!

Little Princess titles are also available as eBooks.

LITTLE PRINCESS TV TIE-INS

Fun in the Sun!

I Want to Do Magic!

I Want My Sledge!

I Don't Like Salad!

I Don't Want to Comb My Hair!

I Want to Go to the Fair!

I Want to Be a Cavegirl!

I Want to Be Tall!

I Want My Sledge! Book and DVD